Birth
and
After Birth

by Tina Howe

A SAMUEL FRENCH ACTING EDITION

SAMUEL
FRENCH
FOUNDED 1830
New York Hollywood London Toronto
SAMUELFRENCH.COM

ISBN   978-0-573-69610-7   Printed   in   U.S.A.   #4298

BILLING AND CREDIT REQUIREMENTS

All producers of BIRTH AND AFTER BIRTH *must* give credit to the Author of the Play in all programs distributed in connection with performances of the Play, and in all instances in which the title of the Play appears for the purposes of advertising, publicizing or othewise exploiting the Play and/or a production. The name of the Author *must* appear on a separate line on which no other name appears, immediately following the title and *must* appear in size of type not less than fifty percent of the size of the title type.

BIRTH AND AFTER BIRTH was originally produced by the Wilma Theater, Philadelphia, PA, on September 13, 1995 under the direction of Paul Berman with the following cast:

SANDY..Kate Skinner
BILL...David Ingram
NICKY..Rob Leo Roy
MIA..Jessica Sager
JEFFERY......................................Greg Wood

BIRTH AND AFTER BIRTH was subsequently produced by Woolly Mammoth Theatre Company, Washington, DC on March 27, 1996 under the direction of Howard Shalwitz with the following cast:

SANDY........................Lee Mikeska Gardner
BILL.........................Mitchell Hérbert
NICKY..Hugh Nees
MIA..Hanna Klein
JEFFERY......................................Buzz Mauro

A revised version of *BIRTH AND AFTER BIRTH* was produced by the Atlantic Theater Company, New York, NY, on October 3rd, 2006 under the direction of Christian Parker with the following cast:

SANDY......................................Maggie Kiley
BILL.......................................Jeff Binder
NICKY......................................Jordan Gelber
MIA..Kate Blumberg
JEFFERY....................................Peter Benson

CHARACTERS

SANDY APPLE: the mommy, 30's

BILL APPLE: the daddy, 30's

NICKY: their 4-year-old son, played by an adult

MIA FREED: an anthropologist, 30's

JEFFREY FREED: her husband, also an
    anthropologist, 40's

AUTHOR'S NOTE

AT LONG LAST…
The final draft of *Birth and After Birth.*
And it only took thirty four years to finish!
God bless the Atlantic Theater Company for having the courage to open their 2006-07season with it! Dear old *Birth and After Birth*… which tends to make critics see red and audiences laugh their heads off. What is it about this play that's so divisive? The subject matter for one thing – taking on the white hot battle between the women who choose to have children and those who don't. And the buoyant style -- having a large hairy man play a four year old child, then adding a pair of childless anthropologists who wax lyrical about the exotic birth practices they've seen in the jungle, culminating in the wife being forced to go through one herself on the living room floor.

How does a playwright defend this sort of mayhem and what makes her think she can possibly get away with it? First, there was a vacuum to fill and second, there was something thrilling about *trying* to get away with it.

Having been deeply affected by Eugène Ionesco who exploded social and political rituals in the l950s and '60s, I felt the need to do the same with the female variety. And what sits, or I should say *floats* at the core of a woman's body, detonating the most sacred ritual of all?

All those frisky eggs!

Nothing, but *nothing* is more dramatic than having a baby and watching it grow. Most plays are about family anyway, so why not explore how a couple becomes a family in the first place?

The year was 1971, the feminist movement was in high gear and since there were few dramatic models to follow, the sky was the limit. I could cast a large hairy man to play a four year old, because four year olds are the size of large hairy men, and I could spend an entire act showing an exhausted mommy and daddy getting ready for his party, because that's how long it takes! I wasn't indulging in absurd liberties, I was holding a mirror up to nature.

I worked on the play for two years and then submitted it to my agent. Every self respecting theater in the country turned it down. The only person who got it was Honor Moore, who published it in her anthology, *The New Women's Theatre* in 1977. The message was clear, artistic directors weren't ready for this, so I covered my bare hands with white gloves and turned to the gentler rituals of the charming but doomed Wasps I'd grown up with. No more ersatz birth scenes on the rug, but cocktails in Boston townhouses, walks along misty beaches and giddy afternoons of croquet. From time to time, I'd get requests to do "Birth and After Birth", but I knew the havoc it would unleash. I also knew I hadn't written a proper ending, so I wouldn't let it out.

Twenty years passed. Then three calls came within weeks of each other in the spring of 1995. Paul Berman expressed interest in directing the play at the Wilma Theater, I was invited to work on it at the CSU Summer Arts program at Humboldt State University and Howard Shalwitz called from the Woolly Mammoth Theater asking if he could direct and produce it.

Its time had suddenly come!

So I peeled off my white gloves and strode back into the ring!

With the promise of two productions, I finally nailed the ending. The play had its world premiere at the Wilma Theater on September 13, 1995, and its Washington premiere five months and more rewrites later. Then good old

Samuel French published the acting edition in 1997 and I figured that was that, but not so…

Christian Parker, the Associate Artistic Director at the Atlantic Theater Company, had always been a huge fan of the play, directing not one, but two readings over the years. In August of 2006, I got the fateful call from Neil Pepe, Artistic Director of the theater, saying he wanted to open his upcoming season with it.

"But I'll be skinned alive by the New York Times". You can't do this to me!", I cried.

"But I love the play. It speaks to me and my generation.", he said.

"Where's your fighting spirit? Plus, Christian will direct it."

This was starting to get scary!

But it made total sense, since the Atlantic had opened their season three years before with my translations of Ionesco's *The Bald Soprano* and *The Lesson*. I knew the ending was in place, but was worried about the excess of absurdist mannerisms. I clearly had cutting to do, as well as dignifying some of the zanier moments. So, it was back to the drawing board, not to do a rewrite, but take responsibility. The action of the play is exactly the same as it appeared in that 1977 anthology, it just goes deeper.

So, here at last is the final version, unless some opera composer comes along and asks me to write a libretto.

—Tina Howe

For Christian Parker

ACT I

(The Apple's living room, a surreal but spare blend of suburbia and something wilder. There's the usual sofa, dining area and armoire, but trees are looming in the distance as if one day the house could be swallowed up by a jungle. Today is Nicky's fourth birthday so the place is decorated with crepe paper streamers and balloons. An oversized HAPPY BIRTH-DAY banner crisscrosses the ceiling. But none of this is quite visible since it's 4:30 in the morning and still dark. SANDY and BILL are in their bathrobes, racing to get everything ready before NICKY gets up. BILL shakes a tambourine.)

BILL. God I love tambourines!

SANDY. Shhhhh!

BILL. They kill me!

SANDY. Not so loud.

BILL. What is it about tambourines?

SANDY. Bill...

BILL. *(Shaking it with rising enthusiasm)* They bring out the gypsy in me!

SANDY. You'll wake him up. How often does your only child turn four?

BILL. *(Singing the tune from Carmen)* "Toreadora, don't spit on the flora... Use the cuspidora, that's what its fora..."

SANDY. At least you got some sleep last night.

11

BILL. If I had my life to live over, I'd be a tambourine virtuoso.

SANDY. I haven't even started wrapping the masks yet.

BILL. Imagine being the greatest tambourine virtuoso in the world.

SANDY. To say nothing about all his new musical instruments … drums and kazoos…

BILL. *(Starting to dance)* Concerts on every continent.

SANDY. Horns and harmonicas…

BILL. Europe, Australia, South America...

SANDY. Zithers and triangles...

BILL. Africa, Greenland, Pago-Pago… THEY'D GO CRAZY FOR ME IN PAGO-PAGO! Rip off all my clothes and worship me!

SANDY. Not so fast! What about me?

BILL. What *about* you?

SANDY. What am *I* supposed to do while you're being worshipped in Pago-Pago? *(Long pause)* I'm waiting…

BILL. *(Reaching for her)* Why, you'll be dancing *with* me, silly girl.

SANDY. *(Pulling away)* Woa … Just a minute, buster! What if I want to dance *alone? (Lowering her voice)* In… *Salamanca!*

(She launches into a lively flamenco number sticking a rose between her teeth.)

BILL. *(Astonished)* Honey?!

SANDY. *(Grabbing some unwrapped castanets)* What if I want to turn a few heads on my *own?*

BILL. What's come over you?

SANDY. *(More and more into it, in a Spanish accent)* Exhaustion, Don José de la Madre Mia … I am so tired I am not myself, but a wild thing!

BILL. *(Grabbing her)* DANCE WITH ME, CARMELITA! The night is young and the moon … she is high!

(They dance, stomping and yelping. Then NICKY bursts in.)

NICKY. *(Tearing around the room in his pajamas)* PRESENTS, PRESENTS, WHERE'S MY PRESENTS?

SANDY. *(Jumping out of BILL's arms)* Oh Nicky, you scared me! We were just...

NICKY. Presents, presents, where's my presents?

SANDY. Mommy and Daddy have been up all night getting everything ready for Nicky's party. Does Nicky want to see what they've done? Does he? One, two, three...

(SANDY flips on the lights revealing the birthday banner and balloons. NICKY's stopped in his tracks)

NICKY. Wow!

BILL. Don't make a move until Daddy gets his video camera!

SANDY. Just look at you, Mommy's great big four year old!

BILL. *(Turning his camera on)* I'll bet you never expected anything like this, old buddy, did you? You never dreamed it would be like this!

NICKY. *(Racing around the room)* Presents, presents! Where's my presents?

BILL. Daddy's present to Nicky is a whole video of Nicky's birthday.

SANDY. Such a big boy... It seems like only yesterday I was

bringing him home from the hospital.

NICKY. There they are! *(Finding his presents and diving in head first)* Presents! Presents! Ooooooooooh, look at all my presents!

BILL. Keep it up, Nick, you're doing great, just beautiful ... beautiful.

SANDY. Nicky, you're not supposed to open presents now. Presents after cards, you know that's the way we do it!

(SANDY starts picking up the shredded wrapping as NICKY tears open a series of toy instruments which he plays with rising abandon—drums, guitars, triangles, plastic horns, harmonicas, zithers. etc.)

BILL. *(Filming)* Atta boy, Nick, show 'em how good you can play.

SANDY. Nicky, I asked you to wait. We do cards first, that way we avoid all this mess at the beginning.

BILL. Over this way ... look at Daddy. Oh, Nicholas, are we making a hell of a video!

NICKY. A red wagon!

(NICKY pulls the wagon around the room in raptures.)

BILL. Towards Daddy, honey, come towards Daddy. Oh, Christ, I don't believe this kid.

SANDY. Nicky, how is Mommy going to clean all this up? Do you want to have your party inside a great big mess?

BILL. Stop everything, Nick! Daddy just got an idea! Let's get some footage of Nicky pulling Mommy in his new red wagon! *(Carrying SANDY into the wagon)* Come on, Mommy,

Nicky's going to give you a ride.

SANDY. Hey, what are you doing? It's 5:30 in the morning. I haven't even brushed my teeth yet.

NICKY. Nicky's going to pull his great big Mommy present.

BILL. *(Filming)* Too much... Oh, Jesus ... Jesus... Too much!

SANDY. Please, Bill, I'm a mess.

NICKY. Look at Nicky, Daddy. Nicky's pulling his great big Mommy present!

SANDY. I've got to clean up.

BILL. Will you look at that kid go! Don't tell me my son isn't football material!

(NICKY pulls SANDY around the room making hairpin turns. He suddenly sees an unopened present and runs off to it.)

BILL. Hey, where are you going? You were doing great!

NICKY. More presents, more, more, more!

SANDY. My breath smells.

BILL. Hey, Nick, what the hell? You were pulling Mommy and doing great. Now come back here and pick up that handle!

SANDY. You don't care!

BILL. I've got an idea. Let's put some of these presents in with Mommy!

(BILL starts piling presents on top of her.)

SANDY. I haven't even had a chance to pee.

NICKY. *(Throwing his last opened present across the room)* Nicky's presents are all gone!

BILL. Daddy asked you to pick up that wagon handle and pull!

NICKY. I wanted a bunny ... and a puppy ... and a pony! You said I could have a pony for my birthday. Where's my pony?

SANDY. I stay up all night decorating the room, wrapping the presents, blowing up the balloons, making a really nice party, and what does he do? Just tears into everything. Rips it all up! Ruins the whole thing!

(She gets out of the wagon.)

BILL. All the presents are in the wagon, so get over here, Nicholas and pull!

NICKY. You promised me a pony. You promised!

SANDY. And not one thank you. I never heard one thank you for anything.

BILL. I'm waiting!

SANDY. Do you know what my mother would have done if I had trashed all my birthday presents and never said thank you?

BILL. *(Slamming down his camera)* Thanks a lot, Nicky. Thanks for ruining a great video!

SANDY. She'd have flushed them down the toilet, that's what she would have done!

(NICKY gets in the wagon, lies down and sucks his thumb.)

BILL. Jesus Christ, Nicky.

(Silence)

SANDY. He shouldn't be up this early.

BILL. He got up too early.

SANDY. I have a good mind to take you back to your room!

BILL. If you ask me, he should be sent up to his room!

SANDY. Do you want Daddy to take you back to your room?

BILL. You'd better watch it, young man, or it's up to your room.

SANDY. How would you like to be sent back to your room on your birthday?

NICKY. My room?

(Silence)

BILL. He got up too early.

SANDY. Come on, Bill, take him on up.

(Silence)

BILL. The kid gets away with murder.

(SANDY sighs.)

BILL. Absolute murder...

(SANDY sighs. Silence. BILL imitates NICKY's sucking sound.)

BILL. He sounds like some ... sea animal ... some squid or something.

(BILL imitates it again.)

SANDY. All children suck their thumb when they're upset.

BILL. You'll get warts on your tongue if you keep that up!

SANDY. I used to suck mine.

BILL. To say nothing about wrecking your bite.

SANDY. *(Popping her thumb into her mouth)* This one.

BILL. Do you know how much fixing that boy's teeth is going to cost? About fifteen thousand dollars, that's all!

SANDY. I sucked my thumb until I was twenty-two.

BILL. You'll have warts on your tongue and fifteen thousand dollar braces on your teeth!

SANDY. I used to suck it during lunch hour when I worked at the insurance company. I'd go into the ladies' room, lock the door, sit on the toilet, pop it in my mouth and just … suck away. *(Laughing)* It sounds ridiculous, a grown woman sucking her thumb in the ladies' room. Come to think of it, I didn't stop sucking it until Nicky was born. I was still going at it when my water broke. It's funny how that sucking instinct gets passed on from the mother to her child.

(She resumes sucking it. BILL joins her, sucking his. NICKY looks at them, confused. They immediately stop. Silence)

BILL. Four years old... Wow!

SANDY. *(Scratching her head)* Ever since I got up this morning I've had this itching.

BILL. *(Flopping down beside NICKY)* Daddy's made videos of all your birthdays, Nick and number four is going to be the best. The best!

SANDY. It's strange, because I've never had dandruff. When I looked in the mirror this morning, I saw an old woman. Not old, old, just used up. *(She scratches her head again and a shower of sand falls out.)* It's the weirdest thing, it doesn't look like dandruff or eczema, but more like … I don't know … my brains are drying up and leaking. I'm like some punctured sand-bag...

BILL. If Daddy didn't make videos on your birthday, then none of us would remember what you looked like when you were little. Hell, me and my camera were there when you popped out of Mommy with your fist in the air! *(Picking up his camera, shooting NICKY at close range)* Time passes in the blink of an eye, Nick. Take it from your old man, before you know it you'll be crumpled up in a nursing home wondering where your life went. Why do you think I take all these videos? To give you proof you were here so you can see just how incredible you were. I mean, *are!*

SANDY. *(Shaking out more sand)* Look at me! And now my hair is falling out. Poor Mommy's going bald. *(Pulling out a chunk of hair)* When she looked in the mirror this morning, she saw an old woman.

BILL. You won't be one of those lonely old men, but will have videos to entertain you and all your pals at the nursing home—birthdays, Christmases, trips to the zoo... Shit, you'll be the most popular guy in the place! "Have you seen Nick Apple's video of this fourth birthday party?," the little old ladies will say, crowding into your room with their wheelchairs. All for that backwards glance at the radiance of youth.

SANDY. Poor old leaking Mommy... Bald as an egg.

BILL. Someday you'll thank me for this.

(Silence)

BILL. Come on, give Daddy a big smile now. I tell you, when the Freeds see this video tonight, they'll eat their hearts out.

SANDY. Jeffrey and Mia are coming over to celebrate with

us. Jeffrey and I are first cousins, so we have the same grandpa.

BILL. Jeffrey may take good slides, but I promise you he's never seen anything like this!

SANDY. They're bringing you a special present and everything.

NICKY. Presents!

BILL. When it comes to videos, I'm the best.

SANDY. And you know what great presents Jeffrey and Mia give. Remember the Chinese Imperial warrior doll they gave you last year?

NICKY. Presents, presents!

BILL. King of the heap, leader of the pack!

NICKY. I want to make my birthday wish.

SANDY. I feel so sorry for them. I wish there was something we could do.

BILL. It's none of our business.

SANDY. But not to have children...

NICKY. I want to blow out my candles and make my wish!

BILL. You can't run other people's lives.

SANDY. Neither of them wants children!

BILL. Their careers are very important to them.

SANDY. But they're missing so much.

BILL. *(Handing NICKY a wild animal mask)* Hey, Nicky, how about putting on this mask. Come on, give us a roar.

SANDY. Put on the mask for Daddy!

BILL. Come on Nick, run around the room and pop out from behind the chairs.

NICKY. I don't have to if I don't want to.

BILL. I said pop out from behind the chairs!

SANDY. *(Putting the mask on NICKY)* Look at Nicky!

NICKY. I want raisins.

BILL. Move!

NICKY. *(Collapsing on the floor)* Raisins!

BILL. Will you please get him to run around the room and pop out from behind the chairs!

SANDY. Come on, Nicky.

NICKY. Raisins!

BILL. I SAID: MOVE!

(NICKY rises and pops out from behind the chairs, knocking them over as he goes.)

BILL. Easy, easy.

SANDY. Not so wild.

BILL. I didn't tell you to knock them over.

SANDY. Do something, Bill.

(NICKY flops down in his wagon.)

BILL. *(Slamming his camera down)* Thanks a lot, Nicholas, I'll remember this.

(Silence)

SANDY. *(Starts cleaning up)* Just look at this mess!

(Silence. BILL opens his briefcase and pulls out a letter.)

BILL. I wish you'd look at this letter sometime. It came through the office mail last month. I told you about it the other day, remember? It's from Continental Allied. *(Reading)* "Dear Mr. Apple, It has come to the attention of the accounting department that certain papers in the Fiedler file are either missing or incomplete."

NICKY. Hey, Mommy, let's play "Babies."

SANDY. Not now, honey, Mommy has to clean up.

BILL. "You assured us last month that the Fiedler account had been settled, but now it appears there have been certain ... irregularities. Mr. Brill has brought to our attention the outstanding work you did on the Yaddler account."

NICKY. *(Putting on his baby mask)* Babies, Babies! I want to play Babies!

BILL. "Rest assured, everyone here at Continental Allied knows what a delicate procedure that was." *Delicate*? They don't know the half of it! I was smiling out of one side of my mouth and going crazy out the other!"

(NICKY crawls onto the sofa, cooing and gurgling.)

SANDY. *(Joining him on the sofa)* Alright, alright...

(NICKY hands her a mommy-type mask.)

SANDY. *(Putting it on)* Sweet baby...

BILL. These guys I do business with are killers. *Killers!* I've been thinking about assuming a new identity so I can give them a taste of their own medicine. You know, become one of those happy-go-lucky types that stabs you in the back while shaking your hand. I'd cultivate a whole new "casual" look with distressed jeans and designer shoes...

SANDY. *(Rocking NICKY)* Do you know what baby Nicky looked like when he was born, hmmm? A shiny blue fish! Mommy's little trout!

NICKY. I was blue?

SANDY. Of course you were blue! All babies are blue when they're inside their mommies' tummies. That's because there's no air in the plastic bag they live in.

NICKY. I want to be blue again, I want to be blue again!

BILL. I'd change my name to … Forest… No, Jon without the "H"!… No… Charles!

SANDY. Once a baby pops out of the plastic bag, he breathes air for the first time. And do you know what happens then?

BILL. Charles E. Zinn…

SANDY. He turns bright pink! As pink as a seashell!

BILL. I like that!

SANDY. Actually, you were a little jaundiced at birth, so your skin was more gold than pink. Mommy's precious goldfish!

NICKY. I was gold?

SANDY. Fourteen-karat!

NICKY. Son of a bitch!

SANDY. *(Shocked)* Nicky!

BILL. They'd call me Charley E.Z, for short. Good old Charley E.Z, who could sell a blind man a jig saw puzzle!

SANDY. And your little arms were so skinny, they waved every which way. Do you know what baby Nicky's arms looked like?

NICKY. Nicky was such a good baby, all blue and gold inside his plastic bag.

SANDY. French-fried potatoes, that's what they looked like!

(SANDY and NICKY erupt into gales of laughter.)

BILL. How would you like to be married to Charley E.Z.—man about town and salesman of the year? I'll tell you one thing, it would put an end to all of these letters about "professional in-consistency." *(Waiting for a response)* You're not even listening to me! You don't give a good shit if I'm fired! All you care about is playing your moronic baby games with Nicky! I don't get it! I just don't get it!

(BILL storms out of the room. Long silence. SANDY takes off her mask.)

    NICKY. Daddy's mad.
    SANDY. Daddy's mad. *(Silence)* Just look at this mess!

(She starts cleaning up.)

    NICKY. I don't like it when Daddy's mad.
    SANDY. God, Nicky, you have to destroy everything you touch!
    NICKY. I want grape juice.
    SANDY. I don't understand you. One minute you're the sweet baby Mommy brought home from the hospital and the next, you're a savage!
    NICKY. *(Tearing off his mask) I* said I want grape juice!
    SANDY. You don't care if Jeffrey and Mia walk into a shit house!
    NICKY. I'm going to die if I don't have grape juice and then you'll be sorry!
    SANDY. Well, you can't have grape juice. You'll spoil your appetite for tonight.
    NICKY. I want grape juice, I want grape juice, I want grape juice!
    SANDY. Mommy said no grape juice.

NICKY. *(Hurtling into the middle of her cleaning)* Grape juice!
SANDY. *(Shaking him with each word)* Mommy. Said. No!

(Silence. NICKY makes a strangled sound.)

SANDY. Oh God!

(NICKY faints flat on the floor.)

SANDY. Oh God, oh God, oh God! *(Silence)* Billlllll!
Nicky's fainted!
BILL. *(Flying over to NICKY)* What happened?
SANDY. Oh, Bill, help him.
BILL. Quick, the ice!
SANDY. *(Rushing out of the room to get it)* It's all right,
Nicky, Mommy's getting some ice, Mommy will make you all
better.

(She returns and tosses it all over him.)

BILL. Come on, Nicker, move those legs of yours. Let's see
a little action here! Get some water, Sandy! *(She rushes out of the
room and returns with a glass of water which she hurls in
NICKY's face.)* Keep that circulation going! Keep those veins and
arteries open! Come on, Sandy, this calls for artificial respiration.
SANDY. *(Flopping down next to him)* Artificial respiration?
I haven't done that in years.

(She starts breathing into his mouth.)

BILL. *(Pumping NICKY's arms back and forth)* One, two

and one, two… One, two and one two...

SANDY. Isn't that what you do to a drowning victim?

BILL. Faster, faster, he isn't breathing.

SANDY. We should be doing the *Heimlich Maneuver!*

BILL. The Heimlich Maneuver?

SANDY. *(Squeezing NICKY around the stomach)* Ugh, ugh!

BILL. *(Still attempting artificial respiration)* That's for choking victims!

SANDY. *(Stopping cold)* You're right, you're right. I mean that other thing … PDQ … SOS … CRP…

BILL. CPR! CPR!

(They both start pounding on NICKY's chest.)

BILL. Harder, harder! Use some muscle!

SANDY. I'm trying.

BILL. *(Establishing a rhythm)* One, two three, push! One, two, three, push!

SANDY. I'm so out of shape!

BILL. One, two, three, push!

BILL and SANDY. One, two, three, push! *(etc.)*

(NICKY finally opens his eyes. SANDY and BILL sigh with relief. Silence)

NICKY. *(Weakly)* Sing to me.

SANDY. *(Cradling him in her arms, singing)*
"Hush little baby, don't say a word,
Momma's gonna buy you a mocking bird.
And if that mocking bird don't sing,
Momma's gonna buy you a diamond ring."

NICKY. More, more…

(Silence)

SANDY. We got it in time.

BILL. Jesus.

SANDY. What would I do if this ever happened when you weren't here?

BILL. Well, luckily, it only seems to happen when *I am* here.

SANDY. I don't know what I'd do without you.

(Pause)

BILL. Nick Apple is four years old today!

NICKY. It hurts being born.

SANDY. I know, honey, I know.

NICKY. It hurts Nicky's head and stomach.

BILL. So tell me, Nick, how does it feel being four? Do you feel any different?

SANDY. "Four" sounds so old.

NICKY. I feel ... sweeter.

SANDY. *(Hugging him)* Oh, Nicky…

BILL. And what else?

NICKY. Softer.

BILL. You nut.

NICKY. And cuter.

SANDY. Oh, Nickyyyyy.

NICKY. And furrier!

BILL. Furrier?

NICKY. *(Sticking out his hands)* When I woke up this morning, I saw fur on my hands, white fur.

BILL. The kid's got fur on his hands!

SANDY. My baby!

BILL. And it's growing up his arms!

NICKY. Nicky's turning into a furry rabbit.

SANDY. Oh, Nicky!

NICKY. I like being a furry rabbit!

SANDY. My baby! What will we do?

NICKY. *(Sticking it out)* Look, there's fur on my tongue, too!

BILL. Well, son of a gun!

NICKY. And on my teeth.

BILL. We'll have to get carrots and lettuce.

SANDY. *(Lowering her voice)* What will the neighbors say?

BILL. *(Likewise)* They'll never know. We'll keep it a secret.

SANDY. Bill, I'm scared.

NICKY. *(Whispering)* I'll only leave the house at night. During the day I'll hide under my bed eating carrots. Mommy will plant a special vegetable garden out back with nothing but carrots —huge juicy carrots the size of baseball bats.

BILL. *(Grabbing his video camera and filming)* Great, great! Does that kid have an imagination or what?

NICKY. *(Not moving)* I'll drop down on all fours. I'll develop x-ray vision and supersonic hearing. I'll see sunken treasure under the ocean and black holes beyond the sun. I'll be known as … Rabbit Boy!

SANDY and BILL. Rabbit Boy!

BILL. Do you believe this kid? He could direct movies!

NICKY. *(Seeing it all in his mind's eye)* I'll predict earthquakes and avalanches, heat waves and sandstorms. I'll leap over fences and streams, build vast underground tunnels linking the great cities of the world. Cairo, Istanbul, Addis Ababa… I'll feed the hungry and clothe the poor, erase injustice and bring world peace. And when the going really gets rough, I'll put on my cloak and do Rabbit Magic... *(He rises puts on his special cloak and prepares to do one of his magic tricks.)* Watch closely my hands will never leave my arms.

SANDY. Oh Nicky...

BILL. My son... Mine!

NICKY. *(Lighting a fire in a rigged pan, he sings.)* "They asked me how I knew, my true love was true. So I smile and say, what a lovely day. Smoke gets in your eyes..."

(He pulls a toy rabbit out of the flames.)

SANDY and BILL. *(Clapping)* Hooray Nicky! Yea! Bravo! Bravo!

NICKY. Let's play Rabbit Says.

SANDY. Oh, Nicky, not now.

NICKY. Rabbit says, "Raise your hands!"

BILL. Later, Nick.

SANDY. Please, honey.

NICKY. Rabbit says, "Raise your hands!"

BILL. We have the whole rest of the day.

NICKY. Rabbit says, "Raise your hands!"

(They raise their hands.)

NICKY. Rabbit says, "Scratch your nose."

(They scratch their noses.)

NICKY. Rabbit says, "Lift your right leg."

(SANDY and BILL do everything he says.)

NICKY. Rabbit says, "Lift your left leg." Rabbit says, "Stick out your tongue." Reach for the sky! *(NICKY laughs, clapping his hands.)* I tricked you, I tricked you! Rabbit says, "Rub your belly." Rabbit says, "Hop on two feet." Hop on one foot!

(They blindly obey.)

NICKY. You did it! You did it! *(Going faster and faster)* Rabbit says, "Lie on the floor." Rabbit says, "Get up." Rabbit says, "Fart."

(BILL makes a farting noise.)

    SANDY. Not this again!
    NICKY. Rabbit says, "Fart again."

(BILL does.)

    SANDY. I'm not playing, it's disgusting.
    NICKY. Rabbit says, "Fart three times in a row."

(BILL does.)

    SANDY. It isn't funny, Nicholas!
    NICKY. Rabbit says, "Run after Nicky and play Fart Tag."

(BILL chases NICKY around the room, making a farting sound every time he tags him.)

SANDY. If this is the only way you can celebrate Nicky's birthday, it's just pathetic!

(SANDY stares into space as BILL and NICKY start playing in slow motion.)

SANDY. My front teeth feel loose... *(Leaning over, shaking a shower of sand out of her hair)* It's the strangest thing, I've been smelling the sea all morning. We're hundreds of miles away from it, but that bitter salty smell of low tide is unmistakable. I noticed it the moment the sun came up. *(She inhales, shaking more sand out of her hair.)* Nicky, I'd like you to come back to the table and open your cards.

BILL. *(Pulling NICKY into his lap)* Nicky's four!

NICKY. I love you, Daddy.

BILL. I love you too.

NICKY. *(Hugging BILL)* This much!

BILL. My *boy. My* son.

NICKY. *(Squeezing him tighter)* No, *this* much! Uuuugh!

BILL. All mine!

NICKY. *(Squeezing with all his might)* This much! UUUUUUHHH!

BILL. *(Gasping for air)* Easy, Nick, easy…

(Their hugging disintegrates into a wrestling match. BILL starts tickling NICKY.)

BILL. Tickle, tickle…

NICKY. *(Laughing)* Don't…

SANDY. *(Opening a card, reads)*
"This little pony comes galloping by,
With a smile on his face and a gleam in his eye.
Seems it's somebody's birthday, 'neigh, neigh, neigh,'
Somebody special who's four today!"

From Walter and Amy, and look, they sent twenty-five dollars.

BILL. *(Still tickling NICKY)* Is Nicky ticklish?

NICKY. *(Screaming with pleasure)* Stop... Stop!

BILL. I tell you, Nick, we're going to have a great party tonight!

SANDY. *(Thrilled)* WILL YOU LOOK AT THIS! Nicky got a card from Mrs. Tanner, his nursery school teacher, and they have a strict policy of not sending individual cards on the children's birthdays! And ... *(In a sing song, hiding it behind her back)* ... a metronome from your music teacher, Miss Prudenskaja!

(NICKY takes it and turns it on.)

SANDY. It's important for a child to form attachments outside the home.

BILL. Children need guidelines!

SANDY. Spare the rod and spoil the child.

BILL. If they're not given boundaries, they be emotionally crippled for life!

SANDY. I believe in discipline!

BILL. Children learn from observation!

SANDY. Tolerance comes from awareness.

BILL. Self-respect is built on sharing!

SANDY. Reading readiness precedes cognition!

BILL. The child is father to the man.

SANDY. Great oaks from little acorns grow.

NICKY. *(Gravely)* "Let us sit upon the ground, And tell sad stories of the death of kings."

(SANDY and BILL look at him, amazed.)

SANDY. Nice!
BILL. Very nice.

(Silence)

SANDY. Jeffrey and Mia are missing so much. I feel sorry for them.

BILL. It's their choice.

SANDY. But *never* to have children...

BILL. Their careers are very important to them.

NICKY. I love birthdays! What I love most is blowing out the candles and making my wish.

SANDY. What if they changed their minds tonight? With us!

NICKY. Because Mr. Boo told me birthday wishes come true.

BILL. Jeffrey and Mia have been married for twelve years. I don't think they're suddenly going to change their minds at Nicky's party.

SANDY. But what if they did?

NICKY. I know just the wish I'm going to make! And it's going to come true because Mr. Boo said so.

SANDY. Because of what a great family we are.

BILL. What's going to happen tonight is we're going to have one hell of a party and I'm going to show one hell of a video!

SANDY. I don't know, I have a feeling...

NICKY. When can I blow out the candles and make my wish?

SANDY. Imagine being a woman and not wanting to experience childbirth.

BILL. People have different needs.

SANDY. But never to have your own baby.

NICKY. When can I blow out the candles and make my wish?

SANDY. It would be so good for them.

BILL. As anthropologists studying children of primitive cultures, they see a lot of suffering.

NICKY. I want to make my wish.

BILL. Once you've seen babies dying of starvation, I'm sure you think twice before bringing more children into the world.

SANDY. But their baby wouldn't starve.

NICKY. I want to make my birthday wish!

SANDY. They'd have a beautiful baby.

BILL. They're not interested in having a beautiful baby, they're interested in studying primitive children!

NICKY. Mommy, can I make my birthday wish now?

SANDY. *(Angry)* No, you cannot make you wish now, Mommy's talking to Daddy and it's very important. *(Pause)* But how can they understand primitive children if they don't have children of their own?

BILL. Just because I can articulate their reasons for not having children doesn't mean I agree with them!

NICKY. Daddy, can I make my birthday wish now?

SANDY. Well, you don't have to be so pompous about it. People do change!

BILL. It's very unlikely.

SANDY. But it could happen.

BILL. Well, anything *could* happen, but that doesn't mean...

NICKY. *(Whining)* Please, Daddy, can I make my...

SANDY. Shit, Nicky, can't you let Mommy and Daddy have a conversation?!

BILL. Mommy and Daddy are talking now.

NICKY. *(Starting to cry)* No fair, no fair.

SANDY. He's impossible!

BILL. You'll have to wait!

(NICKY cries louder.)

SANDY. Keep this up, Nicky, and there won't *be* any birthday party!

NICKY. Go on, yell at me and be mean, I don't care because I haven't made my birthday wish and when I do, it will come true because Mr. Boo said so!

(He runs out of the room. Long silence)

BILL. Kids!
SANDY. Kids…

(Silence)

BILL. Remember the parties we used to have? One I'll never forget was my eleventh.

SANDY. My eighth was the best. I invited the entire class. It was on a Saturday afternoon and we strung white streamers from one end of the dining room to the other.

BILL. My mother let me invite the whole class. Thirty-three kids came!

SANDY. The girls got pincushions for favors and the boys got yo-yos that glowed in the dark, but instead of having cake and ice cream, my mother made this incredible baked Alaska.

BILL. We decorated the whole place in red— red streamers, red balloons, red tablecloth...

SANDY. When she brought it to the table, everyone gasped. It was three feet high and covered with peaks of egg white.

BILL. Shit, everything was red! My mother even put red-food coloring in the cake.

SANDY. I can still remember the taste, like sweetened snow.

BILL. That was the birthday I got my red bike. And when we'd finished eating the red cake and red raspberry ice cream, we played games.

SANDY. I don't know where we got the room, but we actually set up twenty-seven chairs for musical chairs.

BILL. Darts, ducking for apples…

SANDY. We played it once, then twice.

BILL. Then we set up chairs and played musical chairs.

SANDY. By the fifth round we decided to alter the rules a little.

BILL. But after a while we changed the rules.

SANDY. When you sat down in a chair, you grabbed someone of the opposite sex, and they sat in your lap.

BILL. It was getting boring with the same old rules.

SANDY. And then you had to … had to…

BILL. So you grabbed a girl and both sat on the chair together.

SANDY. You had to, had to…

BILL. And you kissed the girl for as long as you could without coming up for air, and whoever kissed the longest played in the next round.

SANDY. We played musical chairs.

BILL. After the kissing part, we began unbuttoning the girls' blouses and putting our hands inside.

(BILL pulls SANDY onto his lap.)

SANDY. We played it once, twice, three times.

BILL. *(Nuzzling her)* And feeling what there was to feel. Oh, it was nice, it was very nice.

SANDY. By the fifth round we decided to alter the rules a little.

BILL. *(Deftly slipping his hands in her robe)* And each time the music stopped you grabbed another girl and reached down inside another blouse…

SANDY. When you sat down in a chair, you grabbed someone of the opposite sex and he sat in your lap.

BILL. *(Starting to get amorous)* After a while we forgot all about the musical part of the game, and everyone was just lying all over the chairs, kissing and feeling up.

SANDY. I don't know why the grownups didn't…

BILL. Some of us even got our pants off.

SANDY. *(Resisting)* Bill…

BILL. *(And more amorous)* We locked the door and pulled down the shades.

SANDY. Not now!

BILL. Tommy Hartland and I got five girls under the table.

SANDY. *(Still resisting)* We can't…

BILL. *(And even more amorous)* But by the time we got our jockeys off, the girls panicked and were back in the game with someone else, and there were Tommy Hartland and I, horny as hell, surrounded by all these goddamned red streamers and strawberry gumdrops.

SANDY. I remember, my mother made this baked Alaska. It was covered with egg whites.

BILL. Come on, give us a kiss.

SANDY. Bill..!

BILL. Let's be spontaneous for once.

SANDY. What do you think you're doing?

BILL. Live dangerously!

SANDY. But what if Nicky comes in?

BILL. Screw Nicky!

SANDY. I said, no!

BILL. *(Starting a fresh assault)* "A bird in the hand is worth two in the bush!"

SANDY. OK, but make it quick.

(As BILL moves in for the kill, NICKY bursts into the room, draped in Sandy's underwear—bras adorn his head and shoulders, a pair of panty hose is wrapped around his neck and a slip trails from his waist. He's stricken with jealousy.)

NICKY. Mommy?! Daddy?!

(SANDY and BILL scream and fly off the sofa, hastily put themselves back together.)

SANDY. Nicky?!

BILL. You little prick!

NICKY. What are you doing?

BILL. Thanks a lot!

SANDY. That's a seventy-five dollar bra you've got wrapped around your ears!

BILL. You owe me, big time. *Big time!*

NICKY. I want grape juice!

BILL. I never even *dreamed* of going through my mother's underwear drawer!

NICKY. I want grape juice! I want grape juice!

SANDY. That's it! The child's got to be punished.

NICKY. And I. Want. Ice. In. My. Grape. Juice!

BILL. Well, you can't have ice in your grape juice, you

little...

SANDY. *(Shoving a glass of grape juice at him)* Here's your damned grape juice. Without ice. Nice and *warm!*

NICKY. *(Hurling the glass to the floor, breaking it)* Then I won't drink it!

SANDY. *(Rushing for a dust buster)* Look out, broken glass, broken glass!

BILL. Did you see what he did? He deliberately threw his glass on the floor!

NICKY. *(Lunging towards broken glass)* I want to make my birthday wish! I want to make my birthday wish!

BILL. *(Pulling him back)* Mommy said look out!

NICKY. *(Starting to cry)* Daddy hurt me, Daddy hurt me.

SANDY. *(Frantically vacuuming)* It's all over the floor. Don't anybody go near there until I clean it up!

BILL. I didn't hurt him, for Christ's sake, I was just pulling him away from the glass!

NICKY. You did so hurt me, you stupid idiot!

(NICKY kicks BILL in the shins.)

BILL. Oww! *(Shaking NICKY with each word)* Don't. You. Ever. Hit. Your. Father!

(NICKY wails and SANDY keeps vacuuming.)

BILL. Did you see that? You son just kicked me in the shin.

SANDY. If you ever deliberately break a glass like that again, I'll...

BILL. *(Examining his wound)* He broke the skin.

SANDY. That's it! Take him up to his room, there'll be no

party!

    BILL. My own son drew blood.

    SANDY. I'll phone Jeffrey and Mia and tell them to forget the whole thing.

    BILL. You'd better get the peroxide to sterilize it with.

(NICKY lies down in his wagon and makes his strangled sound.)

    SANDY. Come on, Bill, take him up to his room. We're calling the party off.

    NICKY. But what about my cake?

    SANDY. No birthday party for Nicky this year.

    NICKY. And the candles?

    BILL. You can spend the rest of the day up in your room.

    NICKY. What about my wish?

    SANDY. The child has to be punished.

    BILL. It's your own fault, Nicky, we gave you every chance.

    SANDY. We warned you.

    NICKY. You mean, I won't have any party at all?

    BILL. We tried.

    SANDY. We bent over backwards.

    BILL. Maybe next time you'll listen.

    SANDY. It hurts us more than it hurts you.

    BILL. Maybe next year you'll be a better boy.

    SANDY. I asked you to open your presents after the cards!

    NICKY. No party? No wish?

    BILL. We certainly don't enjoy doing this, Nicky.

    SANDY. No party, and that's that.

(NICKY runs out of the room crying. Silence.)

SANDY. God almighty!

BILL. Jesus Christ!

SANDY. What's happening?

BILL. We had a real chance there.

SANDY. Where's my little boy?

BILL. I was cooking with gas!

SANDY. He's getting so big.

BILL. *Son of a bitch!*

SANDY. Or maybe we're starting to shrink…

BILL. He has to ruin everything.

SANDY. I don't understand…

BILL. It happens every time. Every fucking time! *(Pause)* So, what do you say we go back to bed and pick up where we left off?

SANDY. *(A million miles away)* Hmmmmm?

BILL. I said … how about heading back upstairs?

SANDY. May I ask you something?

BILL. Can't it wait?

SANDY. It's important.

BILL. OK, OK, but it better be good.

SANDY. Promise you won't laugh.

BILL. *(Depressed)* Whatever you say.

SANDY. Do you hear waves breaking?

BILL. Honey, we're thousands of miles from the ocean.

SANDY. I know, I know … but… *(Shutting her eyes)* Shhh! Listen!

(She gently nods her head in time with breaking waves. BILL strains to hear them. Silence.)

SANDY. *(Depressed)* Oh dear, I was afraid of that.

(She leans over and shakes a shower of sand out of her hair.)

BILL. *(Sighs)* Hey, we all have our moments…

(Silence)

SANDY. Look at me…

BILL. So, what do you say we head back up to bed?

SANDY. I'm a ruin.

BILL. *(Getting amorous again)* You look so beautiful in the early morning light.

SANDY. This is starting to get scary.

BILL. Your hair, your hands, your skin…

SANDY. I'm like some rotting carcass that's been washed up on the beach … some squid or octopus that's missing half its suckers, or whatever you call those creepy suction thingies…

(She makes weird sucking sounds and jerking movements.)

BILL. Honey…?

SANDY. Wow… Remember when I used to talk?

BILL. "Used to talk?"

SANDY. I mean really say something.

BILL. You just did. You're talking now.

SANDY. That's it. I'm going to try and talk.

BILL. Be my guest.

SANDY. OK, here goes. I'm a mommy.

BILL. Very good.

(Silence)

SANDY. *(Suddenly wistful)* Remember the week before Nicky was born?

BILL. Atta girl, keep going…

SANDY. Remember how he kicked? And how I had this fantasy that he was a trapeze artist doing loop the loops, swinging from one end of my womb to the other … doing double, triple, quadruple somersaults in mid air… I mean, he was going *insane* in there! You saw how my stomach danced! It was as if he was trying to get up enough momentum to swing out into the world. And remember how I'd cheer him on… "Go Nicky … you can do it… Grab that trapeze! I'm right here, ready to catch you! Come to Mommy!" *(Near tears)* And then he did it! With my last push out he flew, with glitter and roses in his hair… And he was born… my boy! *(Long pause)* I'm so tired all of a sudden. Aren't you tired?

BILL. Wiped out.

SANDY. *(More and more exhausted)* There's nothing left.

BILL. I give up.

SANDY. Look at me…

BILL. It's hopeless.

SANDY. I can't move.

END OF ACT I

ACT II

(Around six-thirty that evening. SANDY, BILL and NICKY sit around the birthday table dressed in party clothes. They wear party hats and are making barnyard sounds. SANDY clucks like a chicken, BILL howls like a coyote and NICKY oinks like a pig.)

BILL. One, two, three—change.

(SANDY meows, BILL grunts like a gorilla and NICKY barks.)

BILL. One, two, three—change!

(SANDY whinnies, BILL whistles like a thrush and NICKY bleats like a goat.)

BILL. One, two, three—change!

(SANDY clucks like a chicken, BILL croaks like a frog and NICKY hoots like an owl.)

BILL. Stop! Mommy's out of the game! She already clucked before! *(Faster)* One, two, three—change!

(BILL hisses like a snake and NICKY gobbles like a turkey.)

45

BILL. One, two, three—change!

(BILL grunts like a gorilla and NICKY squeaks like a mouse.)

BILL. Stop the game! Daddy already made gorilla grunts before. Nicky wins!

BILL and SANDY. *(Applauding and whistling)* Yea, Nicky! Nicky wins!

NICKY. Let's play again.

SANDY. You're too good for us.

NICKY. Let's play again!

SANDY. They should be here any time now.

BILL. Is everybody ready for one hell of a party?

SANDY. Oh, Nicky, I can hardly wait!

BILL. They'll eat their hearts out when they see this video!

SANDY. The whole day would be perfect if only Jeffrey and Mia would change their minds about having children. Tonight, with us.

BILL. Sure, Jeffrey takes pictures on his travels, but he doesn't use a video camera.

(NICKY leaves the table and quietly plays with one of his toys.)

SANDY. And it's going to happen, you'll see.

BILL. He's more interested in isolated shots than capturing the sweep of it all … the story!

SANDY. They may have exciting careers now, but what about when they're retired and all alone in the world. If she waits much longer, it will be too late. Remember Diane Oak? Diane Oak waited until she was forty-five before she had Jonathan. Her cervix had shriveled up to the size of a lima bean and wouldn't even open for the birth.

NICKY. What's a cervix?

SANDY. She passed the ninth month, tenth, eleventh, twelfth ... nothing happened. They finally had to induce her in the fifteenth.

NICKY. What's a cervix?

SANDY. When that poor child was finally pulled out by Cesarean section, he weighed thirty-six pounds and had a full set of teeth.

NICKY. *What's a cervix?*

BILL. It's a part of a lady.

NICKY. What part?

SANDY. The part the baby comes out of, sweetheart.

BILL. *(Whispering)* The hole.

NICKY. The poopie hole?

BILL. Not the poopie hole! The baby hole!

NICKY. Where's the baby hole?

(BILL indicates where it is on himself.)

SANDY. I certainly wouldn't want Mia to go through what Diane Oak did. All her female plumbing was ripped to shreds by that child.

BILL. Babies come out of the baby hole and poopie comes out of the poopie hole.

SANDY. Of course they could always adopt, but it just isn't the same.

NICKY. Where's the poopie hole?

(BILL indicates where it is on himself.)

SANDY. How she and Jeffrey can call themselves authorities on children when they've never had one of their own...

NICKY. Does Mia have a baby hole?

SANDY. She's never felt life moving inside her. It's so sad.

BILL. Of course Mia has a baby hole. All women have baby holes.

NICKY. Then why doesn't a baby come out of it?

SANDY. We don't get to travel like they do, we don't have their kind of freedom...

NICKY. Why doesn't a baby come out of Mia's baby hole?

SANDY. And Mia looks younger than me...

BILL. Maybe there is one in there, but it's stuck.

NICKY. *(Laughing)* Stuck in with the poopie.

SANDY. But she's missing the most basic experience a woman can have, and when you come right down to it, all she's left with are memories of other people's children.

NICKY. How does a lady tell whether she's going to have a baby or a poopie?

SANDY. Tape recordings and photographs of strangers.

BILL. Because if it's a baby inside her, her tummy swells up, and if it's a poopie inside her...

SANDY. Slides of foreign urchins eating raw elephant meat. I feel sorry for her.

BILL. We all have different needs.

SANDY. *(Getting louder and louder)* It's pathetic. Trying to have her own family through other people's children and not even American children, but poor, starving...

(The doorbell rings.)

BILL and SANDY. *(Panicked) They're here!*

SANDY. *(Whispering)* Oh, God, they heard us!

BILL. *(Whispering)* Don't be silly, they couldn't possibly have heard us.

SANDY. They heard us.

NICKY. Heard what?

BILL. *(Going to the door)* They didn't hear us.

NICKY. Heard *what?*

SANDY. Shhhhhhhhh!

(BILL opens the door. MIA and JEFFREY enter, out of breath. JEFFREY is professorial. MIA is a fragile beauty. JEFFREY, MIA, SANDY and BILL speak the following simultaneously.)

JEFFREY. *(Shaking hands with BILL)* I'm sorry we're so late. Mia was delivering a paper at an anthropology convention and got tied up with a lot of questions at the end. *(Kissing SANDY)* Sandy, I'm sorry. (*Putting down a slide projector and several boxes of slides)* Here, let me set this down…

MIA. *(Kissing SANDY)* Sandy, forgive us. I was giving a paper at the university and some visiting professors from Manila had all these questions about nutrition and life expectancy. I thought I'd never get away!

SANDY. Mia, it's so good to see you! We were just saying what a wonderful couple you and Jeffrey are.

BILL. *(Slapping JEFFREY on the back)* We were beginning to worry about you, old man. I was afraid a group of cannibals had cooked you up for lunch. Jeffrey and Mia Flambé with a little hot sauce on the side...

(BILL laughs. Silence. Then NICKY, BILL, MIA, SANDY and

JEFFREY speak the following simultaneously.)

NICKY. I'm four today. Four years old.

BILL. *(Kissing MIA)* Mia, you look beautiful. As always. A vision, an apparition, not of this world...

MIA. *(Kissing NICKY)* Nicky... Look at you! Four years old! I don't believe it!

SANDY. Come in, come in, make yourselves at home.

JEFFREY. *(Shaking hands with NICKY)* Happy Birthday, Nicholas. Well, you're quite the grown-up now!

(Silence. Then BILL, SANDY and MIA speak the following simultaneously.)

BILL. *(Leading them into the room)* Come on in.

SANDY. We were beginning to worry...

MIA. Oh, Sandy, look what you've done!

(Silence. Then BILL, MIA, JEFFREY and SANDY speak the following simultaneously.)

BILL. Well folks, is everybody ready for a great party?

MIA. Jeffrey, look...!

JEFFREY. *(Looking around)* Nice, nice. Very nice!

SANDY. Nicky's been so excited...

(They laugh. Silence, then SANDY and BILL speak the following simultaneously.)

SANDY. It just wouldn't be a party without you!

BILL. And wait till you see the video we made... There's

nothing like a kid's fourth birthday!

(Silence)

NICKY. I got a wagon and masks.

JEFFREY. When the Tunisian hill child turns four, he's blindfolded and led into a swamp to bring back the body of a mud turtle for a tribal feast.

SANDY. No!

MIA. If he fails, he's expelled from the tribe.

JEFFREY. And left on the plains to be picked apart by giant caw-caws.

SANDY. How horrifying!

(Silence)

MIA. In the Tabu culture, four is believed to be a magical age. I once saw a four-year old Tabu girl skin a sixteen-hundred-pound zebra and then eat the pelt!

BILL. Son of a bitch!

NICKY. I can write my name.

MIA. Good for you!

JEFFERY. I saw the same child nurse a dead goat back to life.

BILL. Jesus!

JEFFREY. With her own milk!

NICKY. I pulled Mommy in my wagon.

MIA. Bravo!

BILL. And you should see his magic tricks...

SANDY. Unbelievable! *(Gesturing towards chairs)* Sit down, sit down...

MIA. Sandy, everything is beautiful, just ... beautiful!

JEFFREY. It's amazing what you can do with a little imagination and some helium.

NICKY. Mia, do you have a baby hole?

SANDY. *Nicky?!*

BILL. Nicky and I made this great video this morning, didn't we, Nick?

NICKY. Daddy and I made a video.

MIA. What fun!

SANDY. Bill and Nicky are very close. Ever since Nicky was born they've been close.

NICKY. *(To MIA)* Do you have a baby hole?

SANDY. It's unusual to find a father and son as close as Bill and Nicky.

BILL. I wasn't at all close to my father.

SANDY. I was very close to my father.

MIA. I was close to my mother.

SANDY. I hated my mother.

BILL. I don't remember my mother.

JEFFREY. My mother and father were very close.

SANDY. That's interesting, because my mother and father weren't close a all.

(Silence)

MIA. Sandy, this room is a work of art! I've never seen anything like it!

SANDY. Well, how often does your favorite son turn four?

NICKY. I got lots of presents.

MIA. You must have been up all night.

NICKY. I got a wagon.

MIA. I'll bet you did!

SANDY. And birthday cards... Nicky got twenty-seven birthday cards this year, including one from Mrs. Tanner, his nursery school teacher. And they have a strict policy of not sending individual cards on the children's birthdays. You know, they might forget somebody. So naturally Nicky was thrilled to be singled out like that.

(SANDY hands MIA the card.)

MIA. *(Reading)* "Happy Birthday, Nicky. Sincerely, Mrs. Tanner."

SANDY. *(To NICKY)* Mrs. Tanner sent that specially to you, breaking all the school rules.

MIA. That's funny, this looks like *your* handwriting.

SANDY. So cousins, how long will you be with us before you disappear over the horizon on the back of some camel?

BILL. I can see you now—two tiny specs inching across the Sahara desert.

MIA. Her Y's and N's are exactly like yours!

SANDY. *(Entering BILL's fantasy)* Water, water...

BILL. *(Joining SANDY)* Water, water...

MIA. And look at this N. No one makes N's like these, except you.

SANDY. *(Snatching the card away)* People will start thinking you don't like American children, the way you're always running off to interview toddlers in Iceland and Nigeria.

NICKY. I pulled Mommy in my wagon.

BILL. He's very strong for his age.

JEFFREY. One of the fascinating things about the Berbers is that parents regard spiritual strength much more highly than physical strength.

NICKY. I pulled Mommy and all my presents too!

BILL. He also pulled a rabbit out of a flaming pan!

MIA. Almost any Berber child can converse with desert vegetation.

SANDY. No!

JEFFREY. To my mind, there are no children the equal of Berber children!

NICKY. I got instruments for my birthday.

SANDY. *(Lowering her voice)* Miss Prudenskaja, his music teacher says he's a prodigy!

NICKY. Daddy made a video of me.

SANDY. Bill and Nicky are very close.

NICKY. I got masks for my birthday.

SANDY. Nicky and his masks...

BILL. Give that kid a mask, any kind of mask, and he's in heaven.

MIA. We've always been fascinated by masks and the whole phenomenon of taking on another identity.

(NICKY puts on a series of presidential masks and speaks accordingly.)

JEFFREY. Remember those crocodile masks we were given in New Guinea?

NICKY. *(As Lincoln)* "Fourscore and seven years ago, our fathers brought forth on this continent, a new nation, conceived in liberty, and dedicated to the proposition that all men are created equal…"

BILL. And he's off!

SANDY. He gets so excited on his birthday, he's been up

since six this morning.

MIA. Jeffrey and I were given crocodile masks in New Guinea that were made out of a paste of dried insects.

JEFFREY. You had the feeling that if you left one on your face too long, you'd slowly turn into a crocodile as well.

NICKY. *(As Kennedy)* "And so, my fellow Americans, ask not what your country can do for you; ask what you can do for your country."

BILL. You think this is good, you ought to hear his Shakespeare.

MIA. *(Depressed)* I can imagine!

BILL. The kid's got a photographic memory!

SANDY. You know what time he got up this morning? 4:15! It was still dark outside.

NICKY. *(As Nixon)* "I have never been a quitter. To leave office before my term is completed is abhorrent to every instinct in my body."

JEFFREY. He isn't going to go through every American president, is he?

SANDY. Alright, Nicky, that's enough.

JEFFREY. We'll be here all night!

NICKY. *(As Reagan)* "General Secretary Gorbachev, if you seek peace, if you seek prosperity for the Soviet Union and Eastern Europe, if you seek liberalization: Come here to this gate! Mr. Gorbachev, open this gate! Mr. Gorbachev, tear down this wall."

BILL. OK, Nick, let's take off the mask and calm down.

SANDY. The poor thing's exhausted, he's been up all night.

NICKY. *(As Clinton)* "My fellow citizens, today we celebrate the mystery of American renewal. This ceremony is held in the depth of winter, but by the words we speak and…"

BILL. MOMMY SAID:*(Removing his mask)* CAN IT!

NICKY. Give it back, give it back!

SANDY. That's better. Now we can see your sweet face.

NICKY. I want my mask, I want my mask!

SANDY. Oh, let him keep it, it's his birthday.

BILL. *(Giving it back)* OK, but no more monopolizing the conversation, understand?

(NICKY sucks his thumb through the mask. Silence)

BILL. Take your thumb out of your mask.

(NICKY doesn't.)

SANDY. It's the strangest thing, but ever since I got up this morning, I've been smelling the sea. It's scent is all around me. *(She inhales deeply)* It's as if I set sail in a little dingy and am becalmed in the middle of the ocean, bobbing up and down in my house dress. Maybe I'll catch a fish, and maybe I won't...

BILL. Honey?

SANDY. *(Calling)* Here fishy, fishy, fishy... Here, fishy, fishy...

BILL. Sweetheart?

(SANDY runs her hands through her hair, a shower of sand falls out. Silence)

BILL. Tell us again, just how many languages can the two of you speak?

JEFFREY. Seventeen.   MIA. Thirteen.

SANDY. Jeffrey and Mia can speak fifteen languages,

Nicky.

BILL. My maternal grandmother was Canadian and always spoke French around the house.

SANDY. My maternal grandmother was Dutch.

BILL. But us kids never learned it.

JEFFREY. Canadian French isn't considered a pure language, it's a dilution.

SANDY. I'm part Dutch on one side and Swedish on the other.

JEFFREY. Swedish, of course, is an off-shoot of German.

BILL. I'm pure Canadian and a little Irish.

MIA. Gaelic! I love Gaelic! It's like talking with your mouth full of stones.

NICKY. What am I, what am I?

JEFFREY. Gaelic is one of the most ancient languages on earth. It came from the Celts, you know.

SANDY. Oh, Mia, say a few words in a funny language.

NICKY. *What am I? What am I?*

BILL. *(Angry)* Canadian, Dutch, Swedish, and a little Greek, OK?!

(Silence)

MIA. *(Adding clicking sounds and strange inhalations)* Talla zoo zoo feeple zip.

NICKY. What did you say?

SANDY. *(Laughing)* Isn't it a riot?

BILL. *(Laughing)* Jesus Christ!

NICKY. What did you say?

MIA. Happy birthday!

NICKY. Say something else.

SANDY. More, more, say more!
MIA. Dun herp zala zala cree droop soy nitch.
SANDY. *(Roaring with laughter)* Stop, stop!
NICKY. Say it again, say it again!
BILL. Too much!
MIA. Dun herp zala zala cree droop soy nitch.
BILL. And what does that mean?
MIA. Merry Christmas.

(SANDY, BILL and NICKY howl with laughter.)

SANDY. That was Merry Christmas?
NICKY. Say "Nicky is four years old today."
MIA. Ooola oola zim dam zilco reet tree comp graaaaa, Nicky!

(SANDY, BILL and NICKY laugh even harder.)

SANDY, BILL and NICKY. Again, again!
MIA and JEFFREY. *(The clicking sounds and inhalations reaching their height)* Ooola oola zim dam zilco reet tree comp graaaa. Nicky!

(SANDY, BILL and NICKY are apoplectic.)

BILL. *(To NICKY)* How would you like to be able to speak like that?
NICKY. *(Gravely, with the same strange clicking and inhalations)* Lim biddle ree yok slow iffle snee buddle twee rat ith twank.

JEFFREY. *(Translating it)* I stayed. You left. Two autumns.
JEFFREY and MIA. Nice, nice...
SANDY and BILL. *(Stunned)* Very nice...

(Long silence)

SANDY. We always have such a good time when you come over.

MIA. We wouldn't miss Nicky's birthday for the world.

SANDY. Who else has cousins that speak fifteen languages?

BILL. Hey, I haven't told Jeffrey and Mia about Charley E.Z., this crazy guy that works in our office.

SANDY. *(Trying to stop him)* Bill...

BILL. There's a shakedown going on and a couple of the top -level people are being let go. The things they do to try and hang on. Unbelievable. I guess something comes over a guy when he feels his job is threatened.

SANDY. Not now...

BILL. There's this fellow at work, Charles E. Zinn... Charley E.Z. we call him. He recently lost an important account, so word came down that Charley E.Z. was going to get axed.

JEFFREY. I don't think I've ever heard you mention a Charley E.Z. before.

SANDY. *(In a sing song)* Honeyyyyyyy...

BILL. He'd been getting these letters accusing him of "professional inconsistency"—whatever *that* means—So word came down that Charley E.Z. was going to get fired.

MIA. How awful!

JEFFREY. Poor guy.

(SANDY pulls an imaginary knife across her throat with a sound

effect.)

BILL. So Charley E.Z. took action. And where did he take action? At the office retreat up at Devil Mountain State Park.

JEFFREY. Devil Mountain State Park?

MIA. I've never heard of it.

SANDY. Well, you know Bill and his crazy stories.

BILL. Every year Continental Allied foots the bill for a weekend of hiking, kayaking and star gazing in the wilderness. And this isn't just sales, but the entire organization—accounting, payroll, personnel—everyone from office managers down to the bottom feeders in the mailroom. We're talking over a hundred employees, zooming up the highway in a convoy of chartered busses singing old camp songs... *(Singing in a far away voice)* "On top of old Smokey, all covered with snow, I lost my true lover for courting too slow..."

SANDY. And he's off...

MIA. Oh, I used to love that song.

MIA, JEFFREY and BILL. *(Joining BILL in four party harmony)* "For courting's a pleasure, but parting is grief, and a false hearted lover is worse than a thief..."

SANDY. Good old Bill, always the life of the party.

MIA, JEFFREY, BILL and NICKY. *(Also joining in, all swaying)* "For a thief he will rob you and take what you have, but a false hearted lover will lead you to your grave. The grave will decay you and turn you to dust..."

SANDY. *(Overlapping)* Alright Nicky, that's enough!

JEFFREY. "One girl in a thousand a poor girl can trust."

(Silence)

MIA. Well, what do you say we give Nicky our present now?

BILL. Where was I? Oh yes! Charley E.Z. up in wild and woolly Devil Mountain! *Fasten your seatbelts!*

(NICKY mimes fastening one.)

SANDY. We're in for a bumpy ride!

BILL. So we finally reach the camp ground, head off to our assigned spots and pitch our tents. Then this guy from the mail-room hauls out a harmonica and starts playing sad tunes…

(NICKY accompanies him on his harmonica throughout, playing VERY well.)

BILL. A campfire was lit and this … circle of flames leapt into the sky… What with our close proximity to each other all that free booze that's not all that was leaping into the sky, let me tell you! Whoeeee!

SANDY. Honey, there's a child in the room!

BILL. Poor old Charley didn't know what was coming over him. I mean, the guy's married with a wife and a kid! They're very close.

(SANDY groans.)

BILL. The wife's a real looker and his son's a prince. A handful, but still a prince.

(SANDY groans again.)

BILL. And he suddenly finds himself in the *wilderness,*

jammed up against all his co-workers who are feeling exactly the same way.

(SANDY's groans turn into little mewing sounds.)

     BILL. So he decides it's time to restore his credibility on all fronts… He sets up his own personal tent away from the others, puts down a welcome mat and hangs up a little sign that says, "Yodeley-oh-ho-ho."
     JEFFREY and MIA. Yodeley-oh-ho-ho?

(NICKY quickly scribbles "Yodeley-oh-ho-ho" on a piece of paper, hangs it on the door of the armoire and plunges inside, slamming the door behind him.)

     BILL. *(Lowering his voice)* As the loons, frogs and crickets are making whoopee by the lake, Charley unpacks his duffle bag and pulls out a secret stash of masks and wigs.
     JEFFREY. No!   MIA. I love it, I love it!
     BILL. He's been to these retreats before. He comes prepared!
     SANDY. *(Laughing)* Just so you know, our story teller here hasn't slept in over 24 hours!
     BILL. There's a knock at the door…

(NICKY knocks inside the armoire.)

     BILL. Or I should say "flap," since tents don't have doors.

(NICKY makes a rustling sound effect.)

     BILL. And there stands Marianne from payroll. Beautiful

Marianne Dingle with the blond ringlets and killer body...

MIA. And...? And...?

BILL. Charley greets her with a sexy "Yodely-oh-ho-ho" and she answers... *(In her voice)* "Yodely-oh-ho-ho"... The loons, frogs and crickets are going so crazy by now, they can't hear themselves talk, so he shows her his assortment of masks, she points to the zebra head and he puts it on... They rip off their clothes, drop down to the ground, and they're off! *Yodeley-oh-ho-ho!*

NICKY. *(From inside the armoire)* Yodeley-oh-ho-ho...

BILL. Soon, there's a line outside Charley's tent—all sexes and ages—office managers, temps, you name it. And he has a different mask for each one—mammal, reptile, monster and mythic. And this goes on for three nights in a row! THREE!

NICKY. *(Opening and shutting his door wearing a variety of masks)* Yodeley-oh-ho-ho... yodeley-oh-ho-ho... yodeley-oh-ho-ho... *(etc.)*

SANDY. Easy, Nicky, easy...

JEFFREY. He's pulling our leg.

SANDY. That's my Bill.

BILL. Hey, I was there. I heard it all.

(SANDY storms off to an opposite corner of the room.)

MIA. I had no idea office workers could be so ... frisky.

BILL. So ... Charley's hoping his woodland performance will stem the tide of letters about professional inconsistency, but everything comes with a price. The poor guy's wracked with guilt on the home front what with the wife and kids... I mean, Charley's an A1 husband and dad. True blue... So he's a total wreck! Well, you know what they say... Sometimes you have to cut off your nose to spite your face. *(Pause)* Hey, don't look so tragic! I make it up! This is a party! We're supposed to kick up our heels.

(Dead silence)

MIA. Don't you think it's time we gave Nicky his present?

NICKY. *(Opening and shutting the door, putting on different masks)* Yodeley-oh-ho-ho... Yodeley-oh-ho-ho. *(etc.)*

SANDY. Jeffrey and Mia want to give you your present now, honey...

JEFFREY. *(Puttering with his projector)* Nicholas, you've never gotten a present like this!

SANDY. Presents!

MIA. I just hope he likes it, you never know with children.

JEFFREY. I was an only child like Nicky and something of a loner. What kept me going was my stamp collection. I imagined that each one was designed for me personally by someone very special. A man with sad eyes, a woman with six fingers, a boy who heard voices.

MIA. Don't get him started on his stamp collection.

NICKY. *(Opening the door)* Yodely-oh-ho-ho!

SANDY. Nicky, please, you're embarrassing us.

JEFFREY. My favorite was a two cent stamp issued in 1901 showing a daredevil crossing Niagara Falls on a tightrope, but the printers screwed up and he had this ... faint shadow... A dealer recently offered me $250,000 for that baby, but I wouldn't sell it. No way. I used to go up to the attic and pretend I was that shadow. *(Miming it)* The two of us would be inching along our wire, when he'd suddenly get an attack of vertigo and start to slip... I'd grab him in the nick of time, but that would throw me off. So there we'd be ... 5,000 feet above the rushing falls, clinging to each other for dear life, the crowd gasping, flash bulbs popping … but I'd always save the day. Soon it became part of our act. He'd fake losing his balance so I could take over. It's weird… You'd think I would have played the dare devil, but I didn't want that kind of attention. I preferred being invisible. *Shadow Man! (Long pause)* Strange…

(Silence)

SANDY. It's the oddest thing, but one of my front teeth is loose. People don't lose their front teeth, do they?

MIA. The Qua tribe starts out with all their permanent teeth and then at the age of sixteen, each and every one falls out to be replaced by an entire set of baby teeth. It's a complete mystery to dental science.

SANDY. Ugh!

JEFFREY. OK, folks, we're ready to go. Get Nicky, his present is all set.

SANDY. He's always so thrilled to see you.

BILL. *(Knocking on the armoire)* Come out, come out, wherever you are!

(Nothing happens. Silence)

SANDY. Family means so much to him.

JEFFREY. *(Dimming the lights)* The show is about to begin.

SANDY. Oooooh, Nicky, I wonder what it is.

BILL. *(Lowering his voice)* Nicholas, will you get the hell out of there!

SANDY. You're being very rude, Nicky! *Mommy isn't going to forget this!*

BILL. *(Dragging NICKY out)* Now get over here and sit down!

(BILL sits NICKY down. The chairs have been rearranged to face the slide show which is "projected" onto the audience. Silence.)

JEFFREY. *(Waving his hand over the projector and box of slides)* Happy birthday, Nicky.
MIA. Happy Birthday.
NICKY. What is it?
JEFFREY. Your own screen and projector, with slides of children from all over the world.

(JEFFREY starts showing slides of children doing all kinds of remarkable things, the reflected light and color washing over their faces.)

SANDY. Oooooooooh, Nicky...
BILL. What a present!
SANDY. Look, look...
MIA. Jeffrey took them all.
SANDY. They're just beautiful.
BILL. Son of a bitch!
JEFFREY. We figured this would be something he could work himself.
MIA. And learn from.
JEFFREY. It's a whole new world, Nicky. Make it yours!
BILL. Wow! What kind of film were you using?
SANDY. And Jeffrey and Mia said you could keep them!
NICKY. Isn't there anything else?
BILL. Shit, that's color!

NICKY. Something to unwrap?

JEFFREY. All you do is load the projector and then push this button when you want to see a new slide. Your mommy and daddy can help you with it.

NICKY. This is it?

MIA. These are some of the children we worked with last year.

SANDY. Jeffrey and Mia lead very special lives, honey, they travel all over the world studying poor children.

JEFFREY. Oh, look! The Io tribe. They decorate their faces with an iridescent paint made out of powdered giraffe hooves.

MIA. It's very bad for their skin, actually.

SANDY. I can imagine.

MIA. They're extraordinary children. It's said they can fly. Jeffrey and I never saw them airborne, but our guide took pictures of them flying in formation over the Himalayas.

NICKY. I wish I could meet them.

MIA. Well, maybe someday.

NICKY. I don't have anybody to play with.

SANDY. That isn't true. You have Daddy and me to play with, you go to nursery school three mornings a week and don't forget your music lessons with Miss Prudenskaja.

NICKY. I hate Miss Prudenskaja. She's mean and she smells like toe jam.

JEFFREY. Actually, these slides don't represent the most amazing part of our trip last year.

NICKY. I don't have any friends.

JEFFREY. Our penetration into the bush.

SANDY. I didn't know you were allowed!

NICKY. I wish those children could come to my house.

JEFFREY. We penetrated the bush and saw things no human being has ever seen.

SANDY. Tell us everything, everything!

NICKY. I'm lonely.

JEFFREY. We encountered a civilization untouched by the Industrial Revolution. People living in the Stone Age.

(The lighting gets darker and eerie. As the scene progresses the jungle seems to move into the room with distant sound effects of chattering monkeys and parrots.)

SANDY. *Oooooooh, cave men!*

JEFFREY. There are a bush people called the Whan See who are still arboreal.

(SANDY gasps.)

BILL. Jeeeez.

NICKY. I wish I could play with them.

BILL. Ssssshhhh.

JEFFREY. They live in trees and never come down to the ground.

MIA. What was so remarkable was that they were obviously Homo Sapiens and not simian, yet they had this one extraordinary feature...

BILL. Christ, I hope you had a video camera with you.

MIA. A freakish biological throwback.

JEFFREY. Each and every one of them had a tail!

(SANDY, BILL and NICKY gasp.)

MIA. We couldn't believe our eyes the first time we saw them. We'd been cutting our way through deep brush when we suddenly heard this chattering above us. It sounded like children giggling. We looked up ... and there were these ... people ... swinging through the branches by their tails.

JEFFREY. Small boned with delicate features...

MIA. And covered with this silvery down that glittered so brightly we had to shade our eyes.

(SANDY, BILL and NICKY gasp.)

BILL. Did you get any footage?

MIA. And they had the most musical way of speaking ... a kind of sighing almost.

(NICKY picks up a cello and starts playing the first movement of Bach's unaccompanied Cello Suite #1 in G Major.)

JEFFREY. We were afraid they'd run away when they saw us, but they didn't. They just became very still and stared down at us.

(A sudden silence as everyone becomes aware of Nicky's playing.)

MIA. I had no idea Nicky could play the cello so well!

SANDY. *(In a stage whisper)* He's Miss Prudenskaja's star pupil!

MIA. He's really remarkable!

JEFFREY. Check out his *bowing*…

BILL. Go, Nick!

SANDY. That's my boy!

JEFFERY. Talk about *glissando*!

(They listen for several moments in amazement. He keeps playing, but softer.)

JEFFREY. Where was I?

MIA. When we first met the Whan See.

JEFFREY. Right, right... Because they exuded such docility, I reached up my hand to one and said, "We're American anthropologists, we come in peace."

SANDY. What a perfect thing to say!

BILL. Beautiful ... beautiful.

JEFFREY. They became very excited and all started talking at once.

BILL. At least you had a tape recorder on you.

MIA. I've never seen such eyes ... a kind of creamy pink ... like looking into a strawberry parfait.

SANDY. Weren't you scared?

JEFFREY. You see, we, without tails and wearing clothes, were just as strange to their eyes.

MIA. After Jeffrey spoke, I said a few words, and then our guide gave them some chewing gum. Then as a body, they furled and unfurled their long silvery tails and chanted, "Whan See." So we chanted it back.

JEFFREY and MIA. *(Chanting)* Whan See, Whan See, Whan See...

JEFFREY. Then one of them motioned that we should join them. So we climbed a nearby tree and they gingerly approached us, touching our hair and skin.

SANDY. I would have died.

MIA. They were an exceedingly gentle people who had no words in their vocabulary for hate, anger or war.

JEFFREY. We spent an entire week with them.

MIA. It's amazing how fast you can adjust to living in a tree.

JEFFERY. And not once in all that time did we ever see one of them drop down to the ground, even though they could stand erect, run, and even dance on their hind legs.

MIA. You should have seen them dance! They'd wrap their tails around a branch and start rocking back and forth, swaying higher and higher and then suddenly let go, catapulting through the trees like meteors.

JEFFREY. While the older members of the tribe banged on drums made of hollow tree stumps.

MIA. Our last day there they asked us to join them. The leader gripped me around the waist with his tail and started whirling me through the air. Everything was spinning and pulsing... There was this very strong smell about him... Cinnamon, cinnamon dust sprinkled through his fur... He spun me higher and higher and then let go... We went flying through the air ... the speed ... the height ... those sparkling pink eyes... I could feel his heart and taste his fur ... it was just ... I can't even ... I thought I'd ... it was so...

(Silence, except for NICKY's playing. When he finishes he curls up on the floor with one of his toys and goes to sleep.)

BILL. Jesus!

SANDY. Oh, Mia...

JEFFREY. Other tribes in the bush have repeatedly tried to capture the Whan See because of their beauty and grace, but once a Whan See touches ground, they die. Something happens to their center of gravity, their balance goes haywire.

SANDY. Oh, no...

BILL. I just hope you had a film crew with you!

JEFFREY. In spite of their ignorance of science and technology, they displayed incredible artistic sophistication. They did these bark carvings with their teeth that were absolutely stunning!

MIA. It was a form of relaxation. They'd sit in the shade, tearing out the most intricate designs.

JEFFREY. Their virtuosity was astonishing. On the one hand, they did representational carvings depicting familiar bush objects, but then they also did these highly abstract designs that resembled some sort of ancient calligraphy.

MIA. And of course that constant gnawing on tree bark provided them with excellent dental hygiene.

SANDY. I've never heard anything like this.

JEFFREY. They also did exquisite lace work, tearing into large paw paw leaves.

SANDY. You should write a book.

BILL. Tell me you got some footage!

JEFFREY. It's funny about my pictures of the Whan See... Not one of them came out. There must have been something in their silvery fur that set off a toxic reaction to my film.

MIA. The whole thing was like a dream except...

JEFFREY. Except...

SANDY. Oh no, it will be something awful!

MIA. We didn't find out about it until our last night, otherwise we'd still be there.

JEFFREY. Neither of us wanted to leave. We'd have given up everything to stay with them.

MIA. Our careers, our fieldwork, our publications...

JEFFREY. Sometimes at night we'd watch them make love, their silvery bodies radiating a kind of shimmering electricity. And everyone would watch: children, parents, grandparents...

MIA. But that last evening we saw the flaw...

JEFFREY. The sty...
MIA. The moral defect.
BILL. *They eat their young!*

(SANDY screams.)

MIA. Our last evening there a young girl went into child birth.
SANDY. *(Hands over her ears)* I can't listen!
MIA. As usual, everyone gathered around to watch, since they had no concept of privacy or modesty.
JEFFREY. No one doctor or midwife was in charge—the delivery was the responsibility of all the women of the tribe.
MIA. As the girl was in the final throes of labor, the older women reached out their hands to help her.
SANDY. It will be awful!
MIA. Finally her moment came, the head appeared. She gave a shrill yelp of pain and joy.

(SANDY gasps.)

MIA. And the baby was born.
SANDY. Thank God!
MIA. But the very instant it emerged, they lifted the tiny creature up and ... and...
SANDY. *(Hands flying to her heart)* Don't!
MIA. It's too awful.
BILL. *One of the elders popped it in his mouth!*

(SANDY screams.)

MIA. They lifted the tiny creature up and reinserted it back into its mother's womb.

SANDY and BILL. But that's impossible!

MIA. And they did it again and again and again and again...

BILL. Son of a bitch!

MIA. And the mother kept urging them on. As soon as the baby came out, she'd motion them to ... stuff him back in. It was obviously some sort of ritual. There was a minimal number of reinsertions the mother had to withstand.

SANDY. I don't believe it! It's unnatural.

BILL. Did. You. Get. Any. Footage?

JEFFREY. Only the strongest survive.

BILL. If you got any of that on tape, you could make one hell of a documentary!

SANDY. But why? Why did she do it?

JEFFREY. You have to remember, these were a highly primitive people who took things literally. When a civilized woman has a baby, she too is possessive, only in more subtle ways. She's possessive of her birth experience and delights in retelling it. She's possessive of her baby and tries to keep him helpless for as long as possible. Well, these Stone Age women were just acting out those same impulses by forcing the baby back into the womb. Through fetal reinsertion you see, the primitive mother could experience her moment of motherhood again and again and again.

MIA. After the fourth insertion her uterus went into profound shock, and how that baby squealed. It wasn't human after a while, but mangled ... and drenched ... like some rodent ... some furry little ... hamster.

SANDY. I'm going to be sick.

JEFFREY. *(Moving away from them, holding some slides up to the light)* I've got to go through these slides and make sure I gave Nicky the right ones... Let's see ... oh, yes, Caracas! What's this one of Nepal doing in here?

MIA. After awhile they motioned me to join them and pulled me over to where she lay.

SANDY. I wish you'd stop this.

MIA. It was such a beautiful night, the air was so warm... I didn't understand what they wanted me to do at first, so I just stood there.

JEFFREY. That's enough, darling…

SANDY. I haven't been feeling well today. When I looked in the mirror this morning, I saw an old woman.

MIA. Then someone gripped my hand, guiding it towards the girl's birth canal. I felt something warm and moist. I looked down. I was holding the baby's head. Such a tiny head. It was about the size of a softball and covered with that same silvery fur, except it was wet and matted down. It was so slippery I was afraid I'd drop it, but then this other hand closed over mine and brought the baby up against his mother's birth canal, which opened again, receiving him.

SANDY. I've been smelling the sea ever since I got up.

MIA. Her body convulsed, the baby came out again and again: five, six, seven times...

JEFFREY. You know what happens.

SANDY. My front teeth feel loose.

MIA. After a while I noticed that I was doing it by myself, no one was helping me, I was inserting the baby!

JEFFREY. You get confused.

SANDY. I feel so tired all the time.

MIA. You know what it felt like? Stuffing a turkey. Stuffing a fifty-pound turkey with some little ... hamster or guinea pig.

SANDY. Oh Nicky … my Nicky … just look at him!

MIA. And there was this overpowering cinnamon smell. I started laughing.

JEFFREY. Yoo hoo...? Darling?

SANDY. Nicky is four today. My son is four years old.

MIA. And then everyone started laughing, with those light sighing voices, but then something went wrong. The baby stopped moving.

SANDY. You're afraid.

MIA. It went all stiff in my hands.

SANDY. You're afraid to have a baby.

MIA. The mother didn't realize. She kept motioning me to stuff him back in.

JEFFREY. Enough is enough!

SANDY. You're afraid something will be wrong.

MIA. *(Increasingly upset)* I didn't know what to do.

SANDY. We're all afraid, but *it isn't like that!*

MIA. Everyone looked at me, waiting...

JEFFREY. *(Even more upset, disappearing into his slides)* Don't say I didn't warn you!

SANDY. Of course there are sacrifices.

MIA. Finally, I laid him in her arms. She bared her breast to him, cupping his tiny head against her, but he didn't move.

SANDY. For the first few years you'd have to stay home.

BILL. You certainly couldn't take an infant into some mud village with no sanitary or medical facilities.

MIA. She breathed into his mouth, she slapped his face, she dug at his closed eyes with sticks, no life anywhere...

JEFFREY. You're on your own here! Let's see, where was I? *(Looking at a new slide)* Ah, yes, the Wahai children who speak with their elbows!

SANDY. You'd have to forget about your career for six or

seven years.

(JEFFREY starts making strange gestures with his elbows.)

BILL. Maybe even longer.

MIA. She understood at last and screamed this scream.

SANDY. It isn't like that, it just isn't like that.

BILL. You should have seen Sandy ... natural childbirth all the way.

SANDY. It was great!

MIA. Then in one awful moment, she rose, lashed the baby to her chest, spread out her arms and jumped.

JEFFREY. *(Looking at another slide)* The green eyed hermaphrodites who fixed my glasses! Speaking of which, where *are* my glasses? I must have left them in the car. I'll be right back.

(He exits.)

BILL. She was in labor 32 hours.

SANDY. Thirty six!

MIA. Down they plunged and were lost in the night.

BILL. The woman was magnificent!

MIA. Gone. Swallowed up. *(Staggering)* I don't feel well.

SANDY. *(Trying to steady her)* Oh Mia, *you* should have a baby!

BILL. It would change your life.

MIA. I'm so dizzy all of a sudden.

SANDY. *(Guiding MIA onto the floor)* You'd better lie down.

BILL. *(Helping SANDY)* Atta girl...
MIA. The room is spinning.
SANDY. Take a deep breath. In ... and out. In ... and out. In ... and out...
BILL. *(Attending MIA as a doctor)* Her pulse is racing.
SANDY. Come on, breathe! *(Setting up a rhythm) In ...* and out. In ... and out...
BILL. *(Breathing with SANDY) In ...* and out. In ... and out...
SANDY. Nicky, we need you too.

(NICKY wakes up and joins in with great concentration and flair. He takes blood pressure, administers shots, writes on charts.)

SANDY. Don't worry, we're right here. *We won't leave you*!
BILL. In ... and out. In ... and out. In ... and out...
NICKY. Blood pressure: a hundred and fifty over two hundred and seventy-seven. Heart racing, irregular cardiovascular pattern.
SANDY. Don't stiffen up ... relax and breathe ... relax and breathe...

(SANDY breathes with BILL.)

SANDY. It's the most beautiful experience a woman can have. Breathe in ... and out ... In and out...

(MIA starts breathing in time with her.)

SANDY. Good girl... That's right... Hold it... Let it out slowly...

MIA. *Oh! Something's happening!*

NICKY. Pulse: sixty over eighty. Blood pressure: two hundred and thirty over ninety-eight. She should be dilated about seven centimeters by now.

(They all breathe faster.)

MIA. *(Screaming in pain)* Oh!... Oh! What's happening to me? I don't want this ... please... I... Oh!

SANDY. *(Holding her hand)* You're doing beautifully. The first is always the hardest.

MIA. In and... Oh!... Oh! Help me!

BILL. The first is always the hardest.

NICKY. The first *is* always the hardest.

SANDY. But the most rewarding.

BILL. Certainly the most rewarding.

NICKY. Absolutely the most rewarding!

MIA. Can't you do something? Can't you stop it? God!... Oh! Stop it!

BILL. *(Struggling to hold her down)* You'd better give me a hand, she's fighting.

NICKY. If you don't cooperate with us, you'll have to be put to sleep and miss everything.

SANDY. That's right, you'll miss everything.

BILL, SANDY and NICKY. You don't want to miss everything, do you?

NICKY. Blood pressure: 250 over 6. Lungs congested... I want this woman on a respirator!

SANDY. You've got to relax!

BILL. We'll have to put her to sleep.

SANDY. Push, hold, breathe... Push, hold, breathe...

MIA. *(Screaming)* I … don't… Stop… Please! Oh! Oh! You can't… Stop! Help! HELLLLLLP! I… Oh… Ahhhh… Ahhhh!

(She passes out. JEFFREY rushes back into the room, wearing his glasses. He turns on the lights and the encroaching jungle vanishes.)

JEFFREY. What's going on in here?

(SANDY, BILL and NICKY freeze.)

JEFFREY. *(Rushing to MIA's side)* I SAID WHAT ARE YOU DOING TO MY WIFE?

(SANDY, BILL and NICKY leaping away from her)

    SANDY. Nothing, nothing…
    BILL. We were just…
    JEFFREY. Darling, speak to me!

(Silence)

    SANDY. Well…
    BILL. Well…
    SANDY. I guess some women just can't have children.
    BILL. You can't pass a camel through the eye of a needle.
    NICKY. One man's meat is another man's poison.
    SANDY. A rolling stone gathers no moss.
    BILL. All work and no play makes Jack a dull boy.
    NICKY. No pain, no gain!
    JEFFREY. WHAT THE HELL ARE YOU TALKING

ABOUT?

SANDY. Your pathetic wife!

JEFFREY. Excuse me?

SANDY. The woman on the floor who's afraid to have children.

JEFFREY. "Afraid to have children?" My dear Sandy, you don't have a clue about that woman and her passion for children. Not. One. Fucking. Clue!

SANDY. Sorry, sorry…

BILL. We were just…

JEFFREY. I said, *drop it!*

(An awful silence)

SANDY. So … what do you say we bring out Nicky's cake?!

NICKY. *(Racing to the table)* My cake, my cake, my cake...

BILL. Hats, everybody… *hats!*

(He starts passing out party hats.)

SANDY. *(Approaching MIA)* Rise and shine… It's time to get up.

BILL. *(Offering her a hat)* Mia?

NICKY. She's not moving.

JEFFREY. *(Carrying her over to a chair at the table and setting her down)* Let me.

(MIA sits upright for several seconds and then slumps over. SANDY and NICKY scream.)

SANDY. What have we done?

BILL. *(Lightly slapping MIA's face.)* Come on, Mia … wake up…

SANDY. Oh, Bill...

BILL. *(To SANDY)* Get her some water! *(Lifts MIA up, holding her under the arms)* Come on, let's walk her.

SANDY. *(Sprinkling water on MIA.)* Mia? Mia?

NICKY. She's dead, she's dead!

SANDY. She's not dead, she just passed out. She's not moving, Bill.

BILL. I know she's not moving. What do you think I am, *blind?*

SANDY. You don't have to yell!

NICKY. Mia's dead, Mia's dead!

SANDY. Can it, Nicky!

BILL. Maybe we should lie her down on the floor again.

SANDY. Oh Mia, I'm sorry.

NICKY. You killed her!

BILL. We didn't kill her, she just fainted.

NICKY. I *saw* you kill her!

BILL. She should carry medication!

SANDY. *(To BILL)* Prop her up again, she's so scary this way.

BILL. *(Leaning MIA against a chair)* There!

NICKY. *You killed her!*

BILL. Stop it, Nicky, or it's back to your room!

NICKY. How could you *kill* somebody on my birthday? Even I wasn't that bad.

JEFFREY. LEAVE HER ALONE!

(SANDY, BILL and NICKY jump away from MIA.)

SANDY. I came on too strong.

NICKY. I didn't *kill* anybody!
BILL. *(Raising his hand to him)* Nickyyyyyy!

(MIA slides down to the floor again with a thud. SANDY and NICKY scream.)

BILL. *(Peeling back MIA's eyelids)* Someone get some smelling salts!
JEFFREY. *(In an awful voice) I said, take your filthy hands off of her!*
NICKY. *(Starting to cry)* I'm scared.
SANDY. What do we do now?
JEFFREY. Finish the party so we can go home and forget the whole thing.

(Slight silence)

BILL. Cake! Cake! Let's bring out the cake!
NICKY. I don't want any cake.
BILL. Of course you want cake, it's your birthday. Get the cake, Sandy.
SANDY. How can we eat cake when she's…
BILL. I said, *get the cake!*

(SANDY exits.)

NICKY. *(Crying)* I don't like this anymore.

(JEFFREY carries MIA back to her chair. She slumps over the table again. Silence. S A N D Y enters carrying the cake, candles blazing.)

BILL. Isn't that some cake? Come on ... let's sing!

(BILL and SANDY sing "Happy Birthday" to NICKY. SANDY then sets the cake down in front of him.)

BILL. Come on, Nick, let's hear your wish.

(A long silence)

NICKY. *(Concentrates, takes a deep breath)* I wish I had a brother.

(Then he blows out the candles.)

BILL. Good old Nick, you never know what he's going to say next.
SANDY. My Nicky...
BILL. That's quite a wish.
NICKY. I wish I had ... three brothers!
SANDY. But what about poor Mommy?
NICKY. I want three brothers to play with.
JEFFREY. All children need siblings.
BILL. That's all we need, three more kids.
JEFFREY. It would do Nicky good to have siblings, I should know.
NICKY. I'm lonely.
JEFFREY. The only child is more prone towards psychosis in the later years.
NICKY. *(Stamping his feet) I* want three brothers for my birthday!
JEFFREY. Forensic studies show that 67% of all serial kill-

ers were only children.

SANDY. He's overtired. We shouldn't have let him come down from his room this afternoon.

BILL. Next time you'll stay in your room!

(MIA slides to the floor with a thud.)

NICKY. I want five brothers! No, I want eleven brothers... thirty-seven brothers ... a hundred brothers ... six hundred brothers ... nine hundred brothers!

SANDY. Oh, Nicky...

NICKY. I want nine hundred brothers!

SANDY. But don't we have fun together? We play Babies and Rabbit Says... Daddy makes videos of us.

NICKY. I want nine hundred brothers!

SANDY. I'd like to have more babies, but I can't.

NICKY. Why not?

SANDY. We've been trying.

BILL. Ever since you were born.

NICKY. Is your baby hole broken?

BILL. Not exactly.

(JEFFREY starts packing up to leave.)

SANDY. There's nothing Mommy loves more than having babies, you know that.

BILL. We've been to special doctors.

NICKY. I want someone to play with!

SANDY. They can't seem to find any reason why we can't conceive again, it's just one of those things.

NICKY. I want to share my room with nine hundred brothers!

BILL. They say if the mommy and daddy try too hard the eggs will get scared and run away.

SANDY. "Scared and run away?" What are you talking about?

NICKY. I want a sister!

BILL. *(Under his breath)* You know … the pressure.

SANDY. Like *you're* the only one who feels pressure!

NICKY. Sisters are fun.

BILL. Hey, I'm the man.

SANDY. *Are* you?

NICKY. I want lots of sisters … with braids!

BILL. I'm doing the best I can.

NICKY. I want 900 sisters with long gold braids. Plus…

JEFFREY. The barren women of the Gabon Tua tribe is considered a witch.

NICKY. *Plus* nine hundred brothers!

SANDY. It's just such a wonderful feeling … life fluttering inside you…

JEFFREY. The barren Tot woman is taken out and drowned.

SANDY. *(Near tears)* Sometimes I imagine I can feel you turning inside me…

BILL. We haven't given up, Nicky. We're still trying.

JEFFREY. In Arabic cultures, the barren woman is…

BILL. *Will you shut up?!*

SANDY. When I looked in the mirror this morning, I saw an old woman who could only conceive once.

JEFFREY. *(Lifting MIA up under the arms)* Well, we'd better get a wiggle on, we've got a plane to catch at the crack of dawn.

BILL. You can't leave yet, we haven't shown you our video

of Nicky.

JEFFREY. We're flying to the tip of South America.

SANDY. My hair is falling out and I could only conceive once.

JEFFREY. A tribe of toddlers who can breathe under water is waiting for us. *(Making strange watery sounds)*

(MIA comes to, making little mewing sounds.)

BILL. *(Blocking his way)* Not so fast … you said you'd see our video.

NICKY. I want to see the video, I want to see the video!

SANDY. Just stay another half hour.

BILL. We saw your slides. Fair is fair.

(BILL starts setting up the video.)

NICKY. *I want to see the video! I want to see the video!*

JEFFREY. We have two stopovers, one in Los Angeles and one in Rio. We're talking thirty-six hours in the air.

MIA. *(Rises and starts staggering around the room)* Ohhhhhhhhh...

SANDY. Nicky was counting on you watching with us.

MIA. I feel as if I've been run over by a train!

JEFFREY. *(Shaking NICKY's hand)* Well, Nick, it was a great party. We'll send you postcards, lots of postcards. You can peel off the stamps for your collection. It must be pretty substantial by now.

BILL. You can't leave now, we're ready to roll.

NICKY. *(Through an imaginary megaphone)* Show time!

SANDY. Show time!

JEFFREY. *(Kissing SANDY)* Thanks for everything, Sandy. *(Cuffing BILL)* Keep the faith, Bill.

BILL. You'd better keep the faith, Buddy Boy, it's a jungle out there!

(Silence)

MIA. *(Still lurching around the room)* Ohhh … I'm so dizzy.

NICKY. *(Grabbing her around the waist)* Don't go!

MIA. I just had the most amazing dream. *(To NICKY)* It was about you!

NICKY. Me?

MIA. *(Sitting down)* It was so strange...

SANDY and BILL. Tell us, tell us!

JEFFREY. *(Looking at his watch)* You'd better make it quick, we've got to be at the airport by 4 a.m.

MIA. I dreamed I had a baby ... and the baby was you. But instead of being normal size, you were tiny, only this big. *(Measuring with her thumb and forefinger)* And you were carved out of *ivory.*

SANDY. I love it! I love it!

NICKY. *(Snuggling close to MIA)* More, more!

MIA. You were so small, I was afraid I'd lose you, so I wrapped you in cotton and put you in a soap dish.

BILL. Hear that, Nick? I guess she was hoping some of that soap would rub off on you!

NICKY. Shhhhhhhh!

MIA. Then suddenly I was in the middle of a forest... It was several weeks later and I'd lost you.

SANDY and BILL. Oh no!

MIA. I was frantic. I started scouring the underbrush looking for you. Scary animals rustled around me, but I wasn't afraid.

JEFFREY. *(Looking at his watch again)* Darling...

MIA. Then I saw this snow white cake in the distance. It was ten feet high and blazing with candles.

SANDY and BILL. Nicky's birthday cake...

MIA. It started to glow with a great light. All the scary animals came out of hiding and started walking towards it. They paraded two by two and then the cake turned into a kind of Noah's ark ... this huge frosted ship. The next thing I knew, I was on board, still holding the empty soap dish. I started looking for you again... I raced along the deck and down through the galleys, past the lions, hippos and snakes but there was no sign of you, so I climbed up to the crow's nest and searched the horizon. I could see for miles ... the ocean was everywhere... I gazed down at the ship. It had become very small, small enough to fit in a bottle... It was a perfect ivory miniature just like you. Then I realized... you were the ship, I'd never lost you. Sometimes you were a tiny baby, sometimes you were a cake, but you were always with me... On land, sea, and in the air... You were my talisman, my magic charm ... my boy...

(Silence)

SANDY. *(Moved to tears) Oh,* Mia...
BILL. Woa...
JEFFREY. *(Taking MIA's arm)* Darling...
NICKY. *(To MIA)* I wish *you* were my mommy!

(A shocked silence)

SANDY. *(Stricken) Nicky!*

BILL. What did you say?

NICKY. *(Throwing his arms around MIA)* I wish *you* were my mommy!

(A shorter silence)

MIA. *(Trying to pull away)* Nicky, Nicky...

JEFFREY. Well ... *tempus fugit.*

(Silence)

SANDY. *(Teary to NICKY)* But what about Daddy and me?

NICKY. I want to be carved out of ivory.

BILL. He's overtired.

NICKY. I want to live in a soap dish.

SANDY. We won't have a son anymore.

NICKY. I want to be a birthday cake.

BILL. The poor kid didn't get any sleep last night.

MIA. *(Heading towards the door)* We'd better go...

NICKY. Stay...! Please!

MIA. We can't.

NICKY. Pretty please?

JEFFREY. It's getting late.

NICKY. *(Struggling to hold on to MIA)* Pretty, pretty please? With figs and kumquats on top!

JEFFREY. Our plane leaves in six hours.

NICKY. *(Bursting into a flood of tears)* Don't go! Don't!

MIA. *(Extricating herself)* There, there, be a brave boy.

JEFFREY. We'll send stamps, lots of stamps! One finds consolation in the strangest things these days.

MIA. Good bye ... good bye ... good bye ... good bye ...

good bye…

(And JEFFREY and MIA are gone. Silence)

    NICKY. They left.
    SANDY. They left.
    BILL. Ingrates!
    NICKY. How could they leave?
    BILL. That's Jeffrey and Mia for you. Always on the move. *(Imitating JEFFREY)* "Our plane leaves in six hours…" Big deal!
    SANDY. *(Imitating MIA)* "I haven't even packed yet!" Well, don't forget your smelling salts!
    BILL. *(Imitating JEFFREY)* "Get a wiggle on, darling, the Squawk children are waiting for us."
    SANDY. *(Imitating MIA)* They're half human and half parrot. Their heads and bodies are like yours and mine, but they have wings instead of arms and are covered with feathers ... shocking pink feathers, the color of bubble gum. *(She squawks.)* You should see them flying through the trees! They look like fuzzy pink bedroom slippers!" *(Squawking more)* These are the children Jeffrey and Mia choose to spend their time with. Not normal boys and girls blowing out birthday candles and making wishes, but mutants, freaks... It's pathetic! I feel sorry for them!

(Pause)

    NICKY. Losers!
    BILL. JERKS!
    NICKY. *(Running to the door, yelling after them)* ASS-HOLES!

SANDY and BILL. *(Shocked)* Nicky!

NICKY. *(Yelling louder and louder)* DICK HEADS! BUTT WADS!

BILL. *(Pulling NICKY back inside, shutting the door.)* That's enough.

NICKY. *SCUM BAGS!*

(Silence)

SANDY. What a day.

BILL. Unbelievable!

SANDY. Now what?

NICKY. I want to see my video. I want to see my video.

BILL. Well, shit on them, we'll see it without them!

SANDY. *(Hand flying to her mouth)* Oh no, my front tooth just fell out! Look!

(She flashes a smile with a blacked-out tooth.)

BILL. I don't need some … dried up anthropologist to see my video. He fancies himself this great documentarian, but he didn't get any footage of those fucked up monkey people. Not. One. Shot. All he's left with is his academic mumbo jumbo. There's no gathering in the family room to see a show, no sharing popcorn with Daddy's special lemonade… The guy's an island unto himself. To say nothing of his whacko wife… I feel sorry for them. I really do.

SANDY. I'll have to call the dentist tomorrow. I can't walk around like this. *(Smiling again)*

BILL. *(Dimming the lights)* All right, folks. Ready for one hell of a show?

NICKY. Show time, show time!
SANDY. *(Showing NICKY)* Look at Mommy's tooth, Nicky.
What do you think?

(BILL sings a fanfare and starts the video.)

SANDY. It looks so tiny lying in my hand.
NICKY. Will the whole video be just me?
SANDY. The other one's loose too.

*(Light from the TV screen flickers across their faces. It becomes
    increasingly dappled as if they're at the ocean.)*

BILL. Hey, Nicky!
NICKY. Hey, Daddy!
BILL. Hey, Sandy!
NICKY. Hey, Mommy!
SANDY. Nicky on his fourth birthday… My Nicky…
BILL. Four years old!
NICKY. Look! Look! Look! Look!
SANDY. Smell that air! The sea's all around us…

*(We hear waves breaking in the distance. BILL and NICKY start
    laughing at the screen.)*

SANDY. *(Wrapping her arms around NICKY)* Four years
ago today, you made us the happiest family in the world! Where
did you come from? And how did you get here? *Our* Nicky …
our boy… It's a miracle … a miracle!

*(The lights focus in on them in an endless embrace. The sound of
    the ocean gets louder and louder as…)*

THE CURTAIN SLOWLY FALLS

Also by
TINA HOWE

Approaching Zanzibar

The Art of Dining

Coastal Disturbances

Shrinking Violets & Towering Tiger Lilies
A Garden of Female Delights
Six Brief Plays about Women in Distress

Museum

One Shoe Off

Painting Churches

Pride's Crossing

Eugene Ionesco's
The Bald Soprano
and
The Lesson
Translated by Tina Howe

Please visit
www.samuelfrench.com

Printed in the USA
CPSIA information can be obtained
at www.ICGtesting.com
LVHW012111160823
755399LV00005B/130